FOR WREN — T. H.

Hope is the Thing with Feathers © 2024 Paw Prints Publishing
Illustrations © 2024 Tim Hopgood
Published simultaneously in 2024 by Magic Cat Publishing, an imprint of Lucky
Cat Publishing Ltd, Unit 2 Empress Works, 24 Grove Passage, London E2 9FQ, UK

The right of Tim Hopgood to be identified as the illustrator of this work
has been asserted by them in accordance with the Copyright, Designs
and Patents Act, 1988 (UK).

9781223188164 Hardcover
9781223188171 eBook

Published by Paw Prints Publishing for North American distribution

The illustrations were hand-drawn using pencil, chalk and ink and then
digitally collaged and coloured.
Set in Bodoni 72
Book and cover design: Stephanie Jones

PawPrintsPublishing.com

Printed in China

FSC
www.fsc.org

MIX
Paper | Supporting
responsible forestry
FSC® C144853

HOPE
IS THE THING
WITH
FEATHERS

EMILY DICKINSON

Illustrated by TIM HOPGOOD

PUBLISHING

HOPE is the thing with feathers –

That perches in the soul –

And sings the tune
without the words –

And never stops – at all –

And sweetest – in the Gale – is heard –

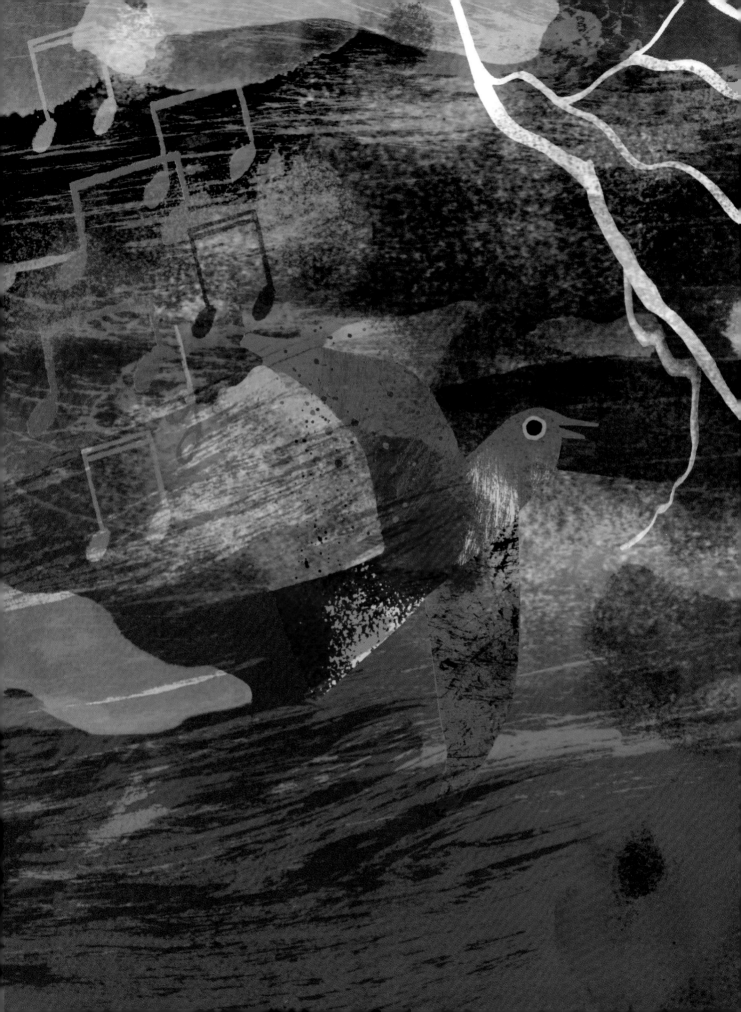

And sore must be the storm –

That could abash the little Bird

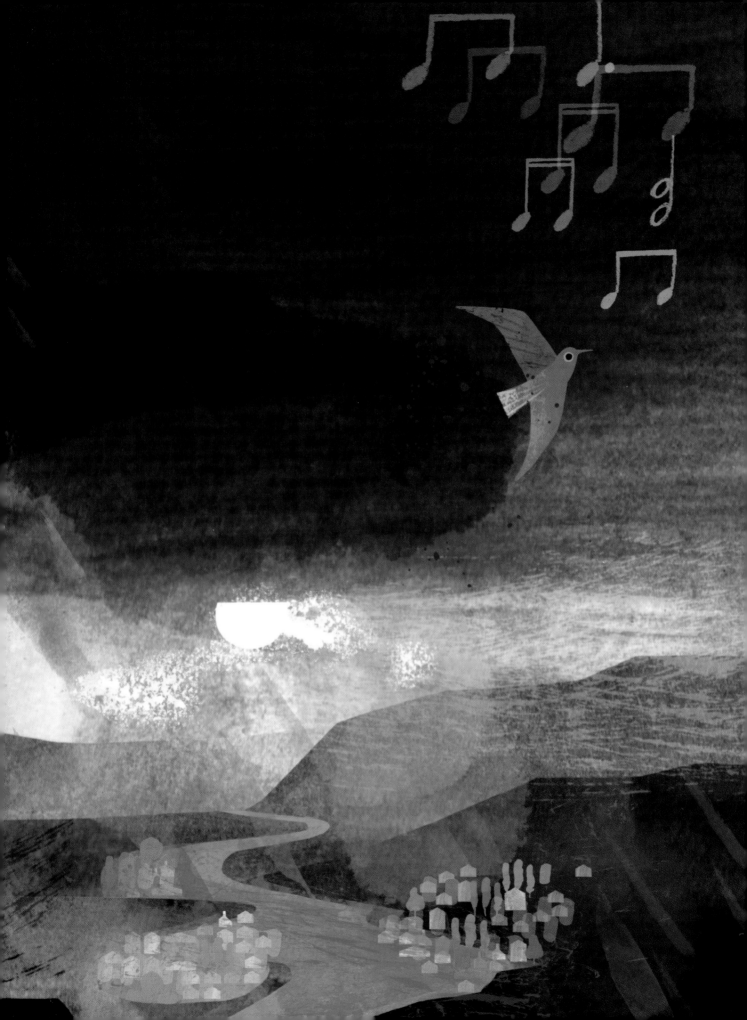

That kept so many warm –

I've heard it in
the chillest land –

And on the strangest Sea –

Yet – never – in Extremity,

It asked a crumb – of me.

EMILY DICKINSON (1830–1886) was an American poet known for writing about love, death and nature. She was born in Amherst, Massachusetts and went to school before returning to her family home. Emily lived a quiet life. When she was older, she rarely left the grounds of her home and had few visitors, spending her time reading, gardening and writing. Emily wrote over 1,000 poems, recording many of them in small, handmade books. Only eleven, however, were published when she was alive.

'Hope is the Thing with Feathers' was written around 1861. In the poem, hope is compared to a bird that never stops singing or asks anything in return, suggesting to the reader that hope can always be found, even in the darkest of times.

Glossary:

Gale – storm
Sore – harsh / terrible
Abash – shame
Extremity – times of hardship

⇀ picture a POEM ↽

Introduce young people to some of the
world's best loved poems, brought to life
in pictures to inspire conversation,
curiosity, and a love of language.

Activity: After reading *Hope is the Thing with Feathers* aloud, create *your* retelling of the poem with your own drawings or paintings. What would you create to represent the poem?
Tag your image to IG @pawprintspublishing

'Poetry is painting that speaks'
— Plutarch, Greek philosopher

Hope is the thing with feathers –
That perches in the soul –
And sings the tune without the words –
And never stops – at all –
And sweetest – in the Gale – is heard –
And sore must be the storm –
That could abash the little Bird
That kept so many warm –
I've heard it in the chillest land –
And on the strangest Sea –
Yet – never – in Extremity,
It asked a crumb – of me.

—Emily Dickinson,
"Hope is the Thing with Feathers"